The
Tiny Turtle
with the
Yellow Specks

Emilia,

may this book bring you joy

as you explore our marvelous

world and follow in the foot

steps of your mom and dad!

Clayton

18. 1. 2017

The
Tiny Turtle
with the
Yellow Specks

* * *

Johann-Caspar Isemer

WIESBADEN, GERMANY

Johann-Caspar Isemer
Adalbert-Stifter-Strasse 46
65193 Wiesbaden
Germany

www.isemer.com

Ordering Information: Special discounts are available on quantity purchases by churches, corporations, associations, and others. For details, contact the publisher at the address above.

The Tiny Turtle with the Yellow Specks / Johann-Caspar Isemer — First Edition

ISBN 978-3-00-053771-4

Printed by IngramSpark

Chapter

Chapter

1

Amanda and her mom were sitting in the park. It was a beautiful summer day! All around them, the birds were chirping and the butterflies were flapping their colorful wings. They sat on the old wooden bench they sat on every time they went to the park.

"Mommy, can I go to the lake?" Amanda asked with big pleading eyes. "I will be careful." Her mom nodded, and off Amanda went.

As she got closer to the lake, she slowed her pace. She did not want to scare her special friend! Kneeling down in the soft green grass, careful not to slip, she put a finger into the water and drew little circles onto the surface.

From below, Jerry noticed a commotion in the water above him.

Jerry was the sweetest little turtle you could imagine. He was tiny. And unlike all the other turtles, he had many yellow specks on his back. He had always had them and he liked them.

But some of the other turtles in the lake made fun of him. They said he was different. They only had green specks of different shades. They said all the bad animals would pick him first because he glowed like a candle in the dark. So he always swam at the bottom of the lake, away from all the other turtles.

There was someone who was very nice, however: a little girl who came to play at the lake quite often. She was always smiling when she looked into the water and saw him swim. Sometimes she waved her arms as if she was swimming with him. He wished that one day, when she was older, they could swim together. That made him smile, and he swam to the surface and peaked his head out of the water.

"Hello, my friend!" Amanda beamed as the tiny turtle looked up at her, with his wet yellow specks glistening in the afternoon sun. Before she knew it, the tiny turtle swam closer and nibbled on her finger as a sign of affection. Amanda cried out of joy. What bliss!

Just then as she knelt there, she caught something furry from the corner of her eyes, hiding under a brush of green a short distance away. A cat perhaps? But no, it had a striped nose and a striped tail! A tiger maybe? She had never seen a tiger around here!

"Mommy, mommy, there is a tiger over there!" Amanda shrieked as she ran back to the bench, somewhat scared. She pointed in the direction of her new discovery.

*
* *

2

Chapter

Her mom turned on the bench – and laughed lovingly. "Oh, that's a raccoon, my dear, be careful! These little creatures look like the sweetest things in the world but they eat almost anything they can get their little paws on."

Catching her breath, Amanda sat herself down on the bench again. She felt relieved that she had escaped "the tiger". To her it still felt like a tiger!

"Speaking of eating, it's time for your afternoon snack." And with that, her mom opened a little tin box. Amanda knew what was in there: carrots. Again! Always carrots! She did not care for carrots very much. "Let's eat our veggies now," her mom said and placed a big carrot in Amanda's palm.

Still in her dreamy thoughts, she replied: "No, I don't want my carrots today." "But they're good for you, my love." "No, I don't want my carrots today!" she said a little louder. "Honey, please eat your carrots..." "No, mommy, I don't want my carrots today!!" she exclaimed, defiantly.

And with that, Amanda raised her arm and threw the carrot towards the lake. In a high bow, it sailed through the air and landed close to the water's edge.

Before her mom could say a word, the raccoon raced towards where the orange snack had landed – and after a few hungry bites, the carrot was gone. Amanda smiled triumphantly. At least she did not have to eat the vegetable anymore!

Just then the head of the little turtle peaked up over the edge of the lake. It wanted to know what all the commotion was about. The turtle's eyes grew wide when it saw the raccoon close by. But it was too late!

In those next seconds, Amanda's tiny heart skipped a beat when the raccoon turned on her precious friend, the tiny turtle with the yellow specks. The furry creature tried to use its little claws to hold on to the shell to carry the turtle away.

"Nooooooooo!" Amanda screamed. "No, no, no, no, not my beloved turtle! Not my turtle! Oh mommy, I am soooooo sorry," and she broke down in tears.

*
  *
*   *
3

Chapter

Further in the distance, a pelican rose into the air. His name was Peet. He had seen what had just happened on the other side of the lake.

That little turtle – that was his best friend, Jerry. They had met once when Jerry had swum into the undergrowth on the far side of the lake. The other turtles had made fun of him and he was shedding little turtle tears. When Peet had met Jerry then, he had told Jerry he need never worry. He, Peet, was going to be his friend. And now he wanted to help Jerry and be there for him!

Even if the raccoon was stronger, he needed to at least try! He recalled what another friend had once shared with him: "Greater love has no one than this: to lay down one's life for one's friends.[1]" That thought made him flap his wings even faster.

As he circled the other side of the lake, Peet heard the wails of the little human he had seen around the lake so often. "Poor girl," he thought, but he needed to tend to his best friend first. As he circled in the air, Peet saw it was Rudy, the raucous raccoon, who was still trying to claw his paws into the shell of the tiny turtle.

After trying in vain for a few moments, the raccoon decided to turn his yellow specked meal onto its back. Yet just as his claws dug under the turtle's body, he felt something above him.

As the shadow of two giant wings cast from on high, he looked up and saw the huge pelican! It was too late for him then. So surprised, the raccoon let go of the tiny turtle for a moment, and "Yiiiiek!" he shrieked in the next. "Ouch! Ouch!" he mumbled as the long snout of the pelican pierced his behind. He turned around and tried to claw at the giant bird but to no avail – the pelican had the upper hand.

Peet had gotten in between the turtle and the raccoon and was now eagerly defending his best friend, Jerry. When the raccoon saw that he stood no chance, he remorsefully rolled to his side and ran away into the bushes.

Not quite knowing what had just happened, the tiny turtle stuck its head out of its shell. When he saw the pelican and that the raccoon was gone, he burst out in joy and relief.

"Peet, Peet, thank you, thank you," the tiny turtle exclaimed. "You saved me, you just saved my life from the big raccoon! What would I have done without you?"

The pelican set his feet down on the soft grass next to him. With his extended wing, he stroked the tiny turtle's back: "That's what friends are for! How are you feeling? Are you alright?"

Still a little shaken, Jerry went still for a moment, concentrating. A few seconds later, he whimpered silently: "I think my belly is hurt. I can feel where the raccoon has struck me with his claws. It hurts."

With remorse in his voice, the tiny turtle lowered his voice even further: "I was only curious for a moment and stuck my head out over the lake's edge. And the next thing that happens is I get hurt. Why am I always the weakest?" This moment of rescue at once seemed like the many moments in the lake when he had felt like a helpless little fool.

4

Chapter

Peet, the pelican, looked at his tiny friend. Jerry was the loveliest little turtle he had ever met, and he had been around this lake for many years. It broke Peet's heart to see his friend hurting as much as he did, both from his wounds but also from his thoughts.

He had an idea. An idea about an adventure.

"Jerry, I know how much you are hurting. Imagine if I told you I have a friend who can heal your wounds. Would you join me on a journey?"

The tiny turtle's eyes flickered. "Ohhh! Is he a doctor?"

"Someone like that, yes," the pelican replied, as his eyes gazed out into the distance, "but so much more, too. He lives a little further away, beyond where the trees are. I know it is a lot to ask of you with fresh wounds: to travel there, we would have to fly."

"We would have to fly?!" the tiny turtle asked with big eyes. He had never done that. He had always wondered what it would be like, to fly, but he did not know whether he had the strength now.

"You know that I love you, my friend! I promise, I will be very gentle," the pelican said. "To fly, you will have to climb into my beak. That will keep you warm and away from the wind up high in the air."

Jerry, the tiny turtle with the yellow specks, wondered for a moment. And then he just said: "Yes." He wanted to see the doctor who could heal his wounds.

As the pelican lowered himself to the ground and opened his bill, Jerry crawled forward on his small legs until he was fully inside Peet's mouth. He was happy to be inside the warm beak of the giant bird. Here nothing could happen, no raccoons and nothing else.

The tiny turtle felt a tingling in his belly as the snow-white pelican pushed away from the ground. He loved having such a good friend.

He was curious about the doctor they would see. Was he another bird, a much bigger one than the pelican? He imagined the white-headed eagle, which he had seen a few times around the lake. Little did Jerry know that Peet's friend Larry was yet someone else.

*
*   *

Back on the bench by the lake with her mom, Amanda looked bewildered at the scene that had just unfolded in front of them.

First the raccoon had come out of nowhere. It had eaten the carrot she had so carelessly thrown away. And then her favorite friend, the tiny turtle with the yellow specks, had come out of the water and gotten attacked by the raccoon! But even that was not enough: then the giant pelican had appeared from the sky. Even though he had chased the raccoon away, then he – the pelican – had eaten the poor little turtle!

Amanda went really quiet and thought to herself: it was all because of her, because she had started it all when she threw that carrot away. If only she had eaten the carrot as her mommy had suggested!

She wished she would be able to get a second chance. She wanted to tell her friend, the beloved little turtle, how deeply sorry she was.

She had no way of knowing that her precious friend was actually alive and well and in the protection of Peet, the friendly pelican.

*
*   *
5

Chapter

U p in the air, Peet was slowly flapping his giant
wings, being careful to shield his friend in his
beak. After some minutes' flight, the pelican
banked to the right and started his descent. He
remembered the ledge in the mountain to land on. It
was just like the first time many, many years ago
when a good friend of his had taken him here, too.
Back then, it was Peet who had been in a similar
predicament as his tiny turtle friend right now.

He landed gently on the stone and peaked into a
cave. Yes, this was it! This was exactly as he
remembered the place. He lowered himself to the
ground again, opened his beak and let Jerry crawl out
from his warm protective cover.

"We're here!" he beamed at the tortoise. "Now, you will be in for a big surprise – just trust me. Come and follow me!"

With that, the pelican staggered towards the entrance of the cave in the mountain. The tiny turtle moved his little legs along, one step after the other, careful not to hurt his injured belly further.

"Larry, it's me – Peet!" the white bird exclaimed in greeting. As he came around the corner, he saw his old friend they had been coming to see. Ahead of them, with an intensely warm and welcoming smile on his face, lay an old lion, slowly lifting his regal head off the floor.

Jerry nearly jumped up. "A lion?" He did not know how to respond.

"Jerry," exclaimed the pelican, "meet my mighty good friend, Larry, the lion. Larry, this is my dear friend, Jerry, the tiny turtle with the yellow specks." Peet looked at his friend and reassured him: "Larry is all you need now. He will take care of you in every regard."

At that, Larry, the lion, looked at the tiny turtle and said: "Hello, my friend! I have been expecting you."

Jerry looked up in surprise: "You have been expecting me?"

"Yes," the lion replied, "but first let me take a look at your wounds. You must be hurting from that ill-behaving raccoon!"

Jerry's eyes went wide. How did the lion know about the raccoon? It was very strange, yet he was amazed. He slowly turned to his side and exposed a little stream of red from underneath his belly.

The lion gently bowed his head, licked the wounds of the tiny turtle and a moment later, the blood stopped running. Jerry felt a tingling in his body and in an instant, his entire broken body had been repaired.

The tiny turtle was astonished. Who was this lion?

As he looked around the cave in amazement, Jerry saw many words written on the wall. He had seen words before on all the signs near the lake. Just like near his lake, he wondered what all those words meant.

The lion seemed to be able to read his mind. "Of course, you are wondering what all the writings are about. They are my diary, words of wisdom imparted by my Father, shared over the last thousands of years. I have waited for this very moment to share them with you."

"I cannot read..." the tiny turtle sighed. "Can you read to me, please?"

"But of course, my dear friend," the lion happily smiled. At that, he slowly lowered himself to the ground and with his right paw gently patted Jerry's tortoise shell. "Are you ready?"

"Yes, yes!" the little turtle eagerly replied.

6

Chapter

L arry the lion looked Jerry straight into his little turtle eyes. With a loving voice, he began reading from the ancient text written on the wall:

"Jerry..."

"You may not know Me but I know everything about you.[2] I am familiar with all your ways.[3] I knew you even before you were conceived.[4] I knit you together in your mother's body.[5] I determined the exact time of your birth and where you would live.[6] Even the very specks on your shell are numbered.[7]"

The tiny turtle looked up at Larry with glistening eyes. "Every one of my specks is numbered?"

"Yes," said the lion, smiling warmly, "because you are so wonderfully made.[8] No other turtle was made like you, and you were made with a purpose. You are loved!"

"I am being loved? Even if I am the only turtle in the lake with yellow specks on my shell?" asked Jerry, eyes open wide in joyful surprise.

"Yes," said Larry the lion, "yes, yes and a thousand times yes! You are loved by Me, and by Him who created all the turtles, all the pelicans, all the lions, even the raccoon..."

"The raccoon?! But... but then why did he hurt me?" Jerry muttered.

"That is a really good question," Larry said. "When you and the raccoon were made, both of you were created with plans for welfare, to give you a future and a hope.[9] The raccoon has indeed gotten off the good track. He has made a lot of trouble lately. However, that does not mean that he cannot turn around. He does have a way back."

"How?" Jerry asked.

Larry looked deep into Jerry's eyes: "I have taken his sin unto me, so that he can be free.[10] You see, we are all offered the same grace and forgiveness for what we have done in the past – and also for the present and the future. Yet it is within our own free will to accept it and act like it."

"Wait! What is grace?" Jerry inquired.

"Another very good question," Larry, the lion, considered. "Grace is a blessing you did not earn or deserve. Grace is lavished on you, without you doing anything for it.[11] It is new life breathed into you by love that cost everything. He who created you loves you that much!"

"Since you were born, you have been adopted by the One who made you, who created you for the very being who you are today. He does not regret making you. In fact, He loves saving you!"

"But if someone made us and loves us, why could he not make everyone be good?" Jerry challenged.

"If your creator were to just force you, then where would be the love? We here on Earth may think that forcing each other to be good is the best way to go... I can tell you, with all His heart Our creator desires nothing more than for us to come home, into His family and into His open loving arms. It is His love for us that He leaves us that choice – to accept it on our own."

"That offer stands for you, Jerry, and for the raccoon, and also all the humans like Amanda, that little girl from the park who always looks out for you."

7

Chapter

H
ow do you know about the little girl?" Jerry
asked astonished. "And how do you know her
name?"

"I just know," Larry, the lion, said knowingly.
"And when you go back to the lake later, I have a
feeling she would love to see you again. She is very
sorry that her carrot attracted the raccoon."

"But I was hurt! What should I do when I see her
again?" Jerry asked.

"Whatever happens to you, put on love.[12] Be
completely humble and gentle; be patient, bearing
with one another in love.[13] Be kind to one another,
tenderhearted, forgiving one another.[14] Let My
peace rule in your hearts.[15]"

"You think I can love her again?" Jerry wondered.

Larry tilted his head and gently stroked the little turtle's shell. "You love, because I first loved you.[16] I have saved you and called you to a holy life – not because of anything you have done but because of grace.[17]"

"Wow! This is like a second shot at life!" Jerry excitedly exclaimed. "Just like Peet coming to my rescue when I needed it most and then you, Larry, taking care of me, licking and healing my wounds when I arrived here. That is amazing! I have never felt so loved."

Larry smiled. "Yes! I have raised you up for this very purpose, that I might show you My power and that My name might be proclaimed in all the Earth.[18] So, as you yourself have been saved by grace, when you go out into the world, love each other deeply[19] – so that through you others may get saved, too."

*
* *
8

Chapter

"Wow! Wow, wow, wow, wow!" Jerry gleamed up at Larry, with a tear glistening in his tiny turtle eyes. "Who are you that you know so much about love and life?" asked Jerry.

"Oh, I am an old lion," said Larry as he gazed off into the distance, "just a really old lion. The lion of Judah.[20]"

"You know, a lot of people are afraid of lions. They think they only hunt and come to rummage and to steal. Nothing could be further from the truth!"

"Think of Me more like a shepherd. I know My sheep, and am known by My own. As the Father knows Me, even so I know the Father; and I lay down My life for the sheep. My sheep hear My voice, and I know them, and they follow Me. And I give them eternal life so that they shall never perish.[21]"

"So you will protect me?" Jerry asked with big eyes.

"Yes, I will," said Larry the lion, a tear in the corner of his own eye. "I want you to know that I have laid My hand upon you.[22] There may be more raccoons out there – that can happen all the time. They will always try to get in between you and whom you love or whom you bring joy to. They will always try – just remember, in the end, we will always be stronger!"

"I want to be with you!" the tiny turtle exclaimed joyously. "When I go back to the lake, I still want to be with you!"

"I would love that very much, Jerry! Before you go," Larry said, "may I say a few parting words over you?"

Jerry beamed at him and said, "Of course!"

"Father, I have revealed You to Jerry, I have revealed You to Peet, and I have revealed You to all the others whom You gave Me out of this world. They were Yours; You gave them to Me and they have heard Your word. They now know with certainty that I come from You.[23]"

"I pray for them: Holy Father, protect them by the power of Your name, so that they may be one as We are one. I have given them Your word. My prayer is that You protect them from the evil one. Sanctify them by the truth; Your word is truth. As You sent Me into the world, I now send them into the world.[24]"

At that, Jerry was speechless. He had never felt so cherished in his entire life.

*
* *
*

9

Chapter

After bidding the lion goodbye, Jerry had clambered back into the beak of his friend, Peet. They flew back in silence, Jerry consumed deep in his thoughts and newfound strength. He definitely wanted to meet the little girl now.

Back at the lake, the pelican landed gently as his feet touched the ground. They were back on the water's edge.

A short distance away, Amanda and her mom watched in astonishment. The pelican had just returned with the tiny turtle, and the turtle seemed unharmed. Even more so: he bounced with joy!

Amanda looked at her mom, and she nodded at her daughter: "Go run, and say hello to your dear friend again."

Without hesitation, Amanda ran to the water. As she approached, she slowed and bent her head in apology.

Looking at the tiny turtle with pleading eyes, she said: "I am sorry!"

The little tortoise craned his neck, looked at her with a huge smile and said: "I have forgiven you."

When tears of surprise and joy streamed down Amanda's cheeks, Jerry beamed at her even more: "Let me tell you a little story!"

"Amanda!"

"You may not know Me..."

Jerry, the tiny turtle with the yellow specks, was now as happy as he ever had been.

ACKNOWLEDGEMENTS

First and foremost, I want to thank my family – my parents, Annette & Friedrich-Eckart; my sisters and their husbands, Lea & Martin, and Charlotte & Tobias; and my grandpa, Herbert – for their countless hours of time, reading different versions of the manuscript, providing feedback and making several critical suggestions to improve this work.

Equally, I want to thank several friends for their time, gracious feedback and helpful suggestions. Thank you Manuel Arens, Anna Bae, Jan Birkhahn, Ulrich Bork, Samantha Cronin, Mariana Felix, Bernice & Pastor Dave Gudgel, Daniel & Tara Fluitt, Chris & Grace Kim, Carrie & Greg Miller, Barbara Philips, Julia Rittereiser, Jonas & Naige Schulte, Timo Seewald, Daniel Ribeiro Silva, Pastor Dan Stockum, Austin Ward, Johannes Wilms, and Ellen Yang!

For her wonderful work on the illustrations that help bring the story to life visually, I want to thank the artist known as 'Yuribelle'.

Many years ago, I got inspired by the *Interview with God* by James J. Lachard and some years later by the *Father's Love Letter* by Barry Adams. I want to thank the respective authors for their positive and encouraging works with Scripture.

Lastly, I want to thank 'colorsinthesun' of Hermosa Beach, CA (U.S.A.) who, unbeknownst to her, inspired me to switch from writing a spy thriller to writing a children's book. You never know how you impact a person's life – you did in ways you cannot imagine and I thank you for it!

ABOUT THE AUTHOR

The Tiny Turtle with the Yellow Specks is Johann-Caspar Isemer's first published written work. Inspired by a California-based children's book writer, he canned his initial plans to write a spy thriller in favor of something ultimately more fulfilling: a children's story with the potential to bring God's love closer to children of all ages who have not heard of His amazing love for us yet!

Caspar was born in Germany, and he works at a technology company in Mountain View, CA (U.S.A.) at the time of this writing. He is godfather to a lovely niece and uncle to two wonderful nephews. He has yet to find his wife.

SOURCES

The citations from the Bible, either cited literally or quoted in the spirit of what was written, have been taken from either the New American Standard Bible (NASB), the New International Reader's Version (NIRV), the New International Version (NIV) or the New King James Version (NKJV) Bible translations.

To read the Bible passages and to further explore the context that these are written in, you can type http://www.biblegateway.com into the address bar of the Internet browser on your computer or mobile device and then easily look them up free of charge.

---

[1] John 15:13 NIV

[2] Psalm 139:1 NIV

[3] Psalm 139:3 NIV

[4] Jeremiah 1:5 NIV

[5] Psalm 139:13 NIRV

[6] Acts 17:26 NIRV

[7] Matthew 10:30 NASB

[8] Psalm 139:14 NIV

[9] Jeremiah 29:11 NASB

[10] 1 Peter 2:24 NIV

[11] Ephesians 2:8,9 NIRV

[12] Colossians 3:14 NIV

[13] Ephesians 4:2 NIV
[14] Ephesians 4:32 NASB
[15] Colossians 3:15 NIV
[16] 1 John 4:19 NIV
[17] 2 Timothy 1:9 NIV
[18] Exodus 9:16 NIV
[19] 1 Peter 4:8 NIV
[20] Revelation 5:5 NIV
[21] John 10:14-15,27-28 NKJV
[22] Psalm 139:5 NIV
[23] John 17:6,8 NIV
[24] John 17:9,11,14,15,17-18 NIV

CPSIA information can be obtained
at www.ICGtesting.com
Printed in the USA
FSOW04n0035281216
28888FS